ON THE RUN

GAIL HERMAN

SADDLEBACK
EDUCATIONAL PUBLISHING

WHITE LIGHTNING BOOKS®

SADDLEBACK
EDUCATIONAL PUBLISHING
www.sdlback.com

Copyright © 2016 by Saddleback Educational Publishing
All rights reserved. No part of this book may be reproduced in any form or by any means, electronic or mechanical, including photocopying, recording, scanning, or by any information storage and retrieval system, without the written permission of the publisher. SADDLEBACK EDUCATIONAL PUBLISHING and any associated logos are trademarks and/or registered trademarks of Saddleback Educational Publishing.

ISBN-13: 978-1-68021-105-4
ISBN-10: 1-68021-105-6
eBook: 978-1-63078-422-5

Printed in Malaysia

21 20 19 18 17   2 3 4 5 6

STATS OF DATING AT EAST LAKE HIGH

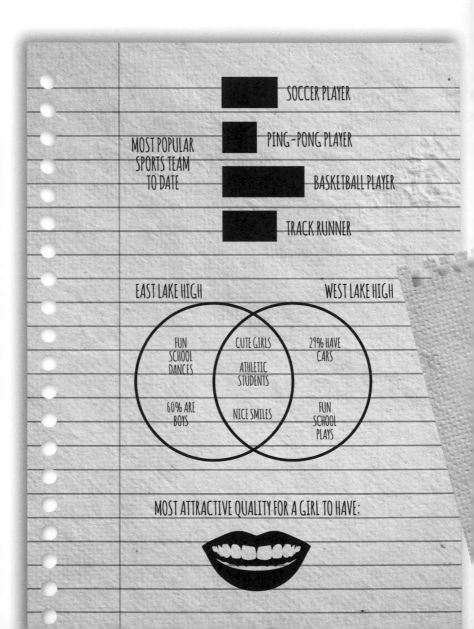

MOST POPULAR
SPORTS TEAM
TO DATE

SOCCER PLAYER

PING-PONG PLAYER

BASKETBALL PLAYER

TRACK RUNNER

EAST LAKE HIGH

WEST LAKE HIGH

FUN
SCHOOL
DANCES

CUTE GIRLS

ATHLETIC
STUDENTS

29% HAVE
CARS

60% ARE
BOYS

NICE SMILES

FUN
SCHOOL
PLAYS

MOST ATTRACTIVE QUALITY FOR A GIRL TO HAVE:

ITEMS IN JACK'S
TRACK LOCKER

CHAPTER 1

TRACK STAR

The sun was shining. A cool breeze blew.

Great weather for running, Jack Porter thought.

Jack was standing at his high school track. All around him runners stretched. They warmed up.

Small tents circled the track. High school banners flew in front of each one. The smell of hot dogs and hamburgers filled the air.

"Testing," said a voice over the loudspeaker. "One, two, three."

The biggest track meet of the season was about to start. Schools from across the state had come to East Lake High. East Lake was Jack's home track. West Lake, the school across town, was there too.

The biggest contests were always between the two schools. Everyone at West wanted to beat East. And everyone at East wanted to beat West.

Jack didn't care about beating West. He cared about beating everyone. For him, this meet was extra important. He was a senior. These would be his last home races. And he wanted to go out a winner.

"Good luck, Jack," one runner said.

Jack nodded. "You too."

"We're rooting for you," said another.

Jack just smiled.

Those guys went to another school. Jack didn't know them. But everyone knew Jack.

Jack Porter was a star. Pretty amazing, he knew. Years ago, no one paid attention to him. Or if they did? They teased him. Kids even bullied him sometimes. Jack used to be a skinny kid. Funny-looking. Back then he just didn't fit in.

In high school Jack wanted things to change. So he joined clubs. He worked on the school newspaper. That helped a bit. He made one friend: a boy named Luke. Luke didn't fit in either. They spent time together. They hung out. But it wasn't enough.

Jack wasn't an athlete. He knew that. But he always loved to run. So he tried out for track. And he found his place. He grew taller and stronger. His straight brown hair turned gold in the sun.

Jack looked different. And he acted different too. For the first time, he felt sure of himself.

Soon, Jack was the number one runner. He made a ton of friends. It became hard for Jack to remember the past. How it was before. How he felt out of place. How he wanted people to like him.

But that was then. This was now.

"Runners! Check in for the mile," the announcer said.

Jack slipped on his spikes. He tied the laces tight. He did one more stretch. Then he stood up straight. He had a race to win.

CHAPTER 2

A RECORD-BREAKING RACE

Jack stood by the starting line. It was time for the mile race. His race. He bounced on his toes. He jumped in the air. Other runners did the same. They were packed together tight. All twenty of them. It was like riding a crowded bus, Jack thought.

Jack grinned. Sure, there were a lot of guys. But he was okay with that. Jack was the favorite to win. He had the inside lane, in front. No one blocked his way.

He glanced at the others. Some frowned.

Some smiled in a nervous way. He turned to the back to look at his school teammates. He gave them a thumbs-up.

Most gave him a thumbs-up too. Luke waved. *Good old, Luke*, Jack thought. He had joined track along with Jack. Year after year, he went to practice. He never missed a meet.

But Luke didn't make varsity until this year. And everyone knew why. Luke was a senior. If you stuck with track? You made varsity your last year. It didn't matter how you ran. You just had to show up.

Jack and Luke were sort of friends. And Jack wanted Luke to do well. He smiled and waved back.

"On your marks!" the official shouted. The runners crouched. The official fired the starting gun. Everyone took off.

Jack ran fast. He wanted to get ahead of the pack. After one lap, he slowed. He kept an even pace. He let one runner pass him. He stayed at the guy's right shoulder.

Let him do the work, Jack thought. *The runner in front uses the most energy. He pushes against the wind. This guy makes it easier for me.*

One lap down. Then two. Then three. The bell rang. One lap to go.

Jack ran faster. Then he ran faster still. He could hear his heart beat. "Go, Jack, go! Go, Jack, go!" he said in time to the beat.

Jack felt strong. He passed the lead runner. A gap opened between them. It grew wide. Jack entered the last straightaway. One hundred meters left. He practically flew down the track. Yes! He crossed the finish line. First!

Jack slowed down. Then he stopped. He bent over to catch his breath. He straightened just as his coach hurried over.

"Four minutes, fifteen seconds!" Coach Brown cried. "A school record! A meet record!"

Coach Brown hugged Jack. Jack grinned. He kept grinning. He couldn't stop. A school record! A meet record! And an amazing time.

Suddenly people were crowding around him. "Congratulations! Great job!" They thumped him on the back. They gave him high fives. Jack peered around them, watching the race.

Luke was just crossing the finish line. Jack thanked everyone. Then he moved closer to Luke.

Luke threw himself on the ground. He breathed hard. But he smiled. "I got a personal record!"

Jack reached down for a fist bump. "That's great, Luke!"

Then Jack noticed a girl. She stood just a few feet away. She was looking right at him.

She didn't go to school with Jack. But Jack had seen her before. She ran for West Lake. Plus she was hard to miss. She was beautiful. She had big green eyes. Her dark hair was pulled back in a tight ponytail. She was tall. Almost as tall as Jack.

She smiled at him. Jack's heart beat a little faster.

Then people surged around him once again. He craned his neck. But she was gone.

Just as well, Jack thought. *I have one more race to win.*

An hour later, Jack was back at the starting line. He was the anchor for the four hundred-meter relay. Each runner ran one lap. Jack was the fourth runner on his team of four. The last one to run in the last race of the meet.

He was set to go next.

Jack's teammate rounded the curve. Two runners were ahead of him.

Jack ran a few steps, holding his hand out behind him. His teammate smacked the baton into Jack's palm. Then Jack really took off. He could pass the other two anchors. He had to.

He picked up speed. Faster and faster. He passed one runner on the first straightaway. He passed the other runner on the curve. He could hear people shouting his name. "Jack! Jack!" The voices grew louder as he neared the end.

He gave one final push. He won!

His teammates went into a group hug. Then Jack stood alone. He wanted to enjoy the feeling. His last high school meet. And what an event!

"Wow!" The pretty girl from West Lake was standing next to him. "You really owned this meet!"

Jack brushed hair out of his eyes. He tried to wipe the sweat from his face too. He hoped she didn't notice.

The girl looked fresh as a daisy. Like she just stepped out of the shower. And Jack? He probably looked like he had run a marathon.

"I had a good day," Jack said.

The girl stepped closer. "A great day."

"Okay." Jack grinned. "How was your day?"

The girl shrugged. "Nothing special. But I have another year. I'm a junior."

"Good job, Becky," said another girl from West Lake as she walked past.

"Becky," Jack said. "Becky the junior."

"I know you're Jack the senior," she said.

She was flirting!

"Jack Porter," she added. "I'm Becky Mann."

Jack saw his parents in the stands. They were heading over. Would he have to introduce Becky?

But she was already walking away. "Got to catch the bus," she said. Then she stopped. "Find me on Facebook?"

"Sure!"

Becky smiled at him. She backed away. Then she ran toward the bus. Her ponytail swung back and forth.

Becky Mann. She looked great. And Jack felt great. All in all, it had been an amazing day.

And Jack felt sure the day would only get better. The first thing he'd do at home? Go on Facebook and friend Becky Mann.

CHAPTER 3

FRIDAY NIGHT DANCE

Jack got home an hour later. He did not turn on his computer right away. He took a shower. It felt good just to think about Becky. To daydream a bit about what might happen. Finally, he went online.

That night, Jack and Becky sent messages on Facebook.

 BECKY MANN   8:17 pm
Do you have any brothers or sisters?

No for both.

JACK PORTER   8:20 pm

What's your best subject?

Math for Becky. English for Jack.

Jack had just sent another one.

JACK PORTER   8:21 pm

What's your favorite movie?

But then a reminder popped up.

SCHOOL DANCE THIS FRIDAY!

Jack didn't like dances. But this one was low-key. More like a get-together, really. He wouldn't have to get dressed up. He could wear a nice shirt. And that would be it.

Besides, this was the last all-school dance. His last one—forever! He hadn't planned to go. But now he changed his mind. He had an idea. The beginning of a plan.

One message later, Becky gave Jack her number. He called her cell. They spoke for an hour. Jack talked about college. About leaving home. Becky told him about her pet bunny.

And how she was going to be a lifeguard in the summer.

It was going great. So Jack put his plan into action.

He cleared his throat. "Are you free on Friday? For the East Lake dance? I know it's only three days away," he added.

Short notice, he knew. She probably already had plans.

"Of course I'll go!" she said.

The perfect end to the perfect day.

It was Friday night. Dance night. Jack drove across town. He pulled up to a red brick home. He checked the address. Yes, it was Becky's house.

For a moment Jack sat in the car. He felt nervous. He barely knew Becky. Sure, they exchanged info on Facebook. They talked for a bit. It didn't amount to much. But she seemed really nice. She seemed interested in everything he said. So he felt excited too.

Jack got out of the car. He walked up the steps. Then he rang the doorbell. He waited. He shifted his feet. Then he waited some more. Again, he rang the doorbell.

Was Becky even home? Was she blowing him off? She had to have heard the bell. It was so loud! He peered through the window. No Becky. He rang the bell a third time.

He heard a noise. It sounded like a window slamming shut. But it wasn't at Becky's house. It was next door.

Becky's door finally opened. She stepped out. She smiled. Jack forgot his fears. "Hi, Jack," she said. "Sorry to take so long."

"That's okay," he said.

They walked out to the car. Becky leaned in close to him. She whispered in his ear, "I'm glad we're going."

Jack put his arm around her. He felt glad too.

A little while later, they walked into the school gym. It was crowded. Music blared. People danced. Disco lights spun in crazy circles. "Do you want punch?" he asked.

"What?"

"Should we get punch?" he said louder.

"I guess."

All of a sudden, Becky sounded bored. Maybe they should have skipped the dance. They should have gone to the movies instead.

Stop it, Jack, he told himself. *Just relax.*

Jack walked toward the refreshment table. He reached for Becky's hand. But Becky pulled back. She walked the rest of the way behind him.

At the table they got their drinks. Becky sipped. She didn't look at him.

"Are you okay?" Jack asked.

"What?"

"I said, are you okay?" he shouted.

Becky shrugged.

Jack felt strange. She wasn't acting like she did by her house. "Do you want to leave? Go somewhere else?" he asked. He was confused.

She rolled her eyes. "No. This is fine."

What was going on?

A few guys came over to say hello to Jack. Then he turned back to Becky. She was gone.

Jack searched the dance floor. Then he waited by the restroom. He checked the dance floor again. No Becky.

He leaned against the wall to think. Over the music, he heard sirens. The sound grew louder. Everything went on as usual. People danced. They talked. Then the music stopped. The regular lights came on. Jack blinked.

Two policemen stood by the DJ table. One grabbed the mic. "No one leave the gym," he said. "Something has happened."

Jack stood up straight. Everyone started talking at once.

"Oh no!

"What's going on?"

"I don't know!"

"It's got to be trouble!"

"Quiet!" ordered the officer. "We need to talk to some students." He glanced at a notepad. Then he looked around the gym. "First person, Jack Porter."

CHAPTER 4

BECKY IS NOT OKAY

Jack froze. "Me?" he mumbled. He couldn't believe it.

"Jack Porter?" the officer called again.

People whispered and looked at him. They moved out of his way. A clear path opened through the crowd. It led straight to the police officers.

Jack took a few steps. His legs felt like jelly. Did something happen to his parents? To his house?

Some kids patted him on the back. "It's okay," a girl said. He kept walking. He reached the DJ table.

"I'm Officer Dale," said the policeman. "And this is Officer Breen." The woman nodded. "Follow me."

"Everyone else wait here," Officer Breen said. "You can sit down. This could take a while."

Officer Dale led Jack out of the gym. "We're going to the parking lot," he said.

"Why? What happened? Did someone steal my car?"

The officer didn't answer. At the edge of the lot, Jack stopped. He saw his car. It was still there. Yellow tape roped off the spot. An ambulance had pulled in front of it. EMTs were bringing out a stretcher. Other officers examined the car.

"Is it Becky?" Jack asked. His heart raced. "Is she okay?"

"No," the officer said. "She is not okay." He spoke in a low, calm voice. Like he was saying he didn't want cream in his coffee. They walked closer. "She's dead."

"Dead?" Jack squeaked.

The officer nodded.

How could that be? *My date is dead*, Jack told himself. But he didn't believe it. She was just standing next to him! Or behind him, at least.

"In fact …" Officer Dale stopped. He looked Jack in the eye. "Becky Mann was killed." He watched Jack's face carefully. He was checking for signs. Guilty? Innocent? Which one was Jack?

Jack slumped against the ambulance. "Becky was murdered?" he asked.

"That's right," the officer said. "Some students left the dance. They wanted some air. They noticed a body slumped in your passenger seat. They called the police. When we got here, the victim wasn't breathing. She was already dead. We checked the plates. And we found out the car was yours."

Jack's mind was blank. The whole thing seemed unreal. Like it was happening to someone else.

The EMTs brought Becky out on a stretcher. They had covered the body with a blanket. But

Jack glimpsed her face. Pale. Hair tangled. And around her neck, he saw marks.

"H-h-ow?" he stammered. "How did it happen?"

"Choked to death," Officer Dale said. "But maybe you can tell us more."

Officer Dale led Jack inside the school. Jack was in a fog. What could he tell the police? Nothing. He didn't know a thing. He barely knew Becky.

The officer took Jack to an empty classroom. It was his English room. Posters lined the wall. Not thinking, he went to his regular seat. It was under a picture of William Shakespeare. The writer looked down on him. He seemed angry.

Officer Breen came in too. "We need to ask you some questions," she said. She turned on a tape recorder. "We know Becky Mann was a junior at West. How long have you known her?"

Jack gulped. "Uh, just a few days." He shook his head. "I don't know what's going on. I didn't really know her at all."

"How did you meet?"

"Wait!" Jack stood up. "Do you think I did this?"

The officers didn't answer.

Jack shook his head to clear it. He'd seen plenty of police shows on TV. He understood some things. He wasn't being arrested. No one had read him his rights.

Yet, there was the tape recorder. Jack knew he shouldn't talk more. But the police kept asking questions. Why was Becky in the parking lot? Did they have a fight? They were accusing him, really!

"Do I need a lawyer?" he finally asked.

Officer Breen shut off the recorder. "You can go. Just don't leave town," she said. "We will need to talk to you again."

Jack flushed. He wasn't guilty. But somehow, he felt guilty. He didn't do anything wrong. Yet he felt like he'd been caught.

Jack sighed. At least he could drive home now.

He took his keys out of his pocket.

"And we need to keep the car."

CHAPTER 5

ON THE RUN

Jack needed to get home. He needed a ride. It shouldn't be a big deal. He could ask someone at the dance. But he didn't want to go back to the gym. He didn't want to face all those people.

He reached for his phone. He could call a friend. Someone who wasn't here. Or his parents. His mom and dad would be here in ten minutes. But he wasn't ready to talk to anyone. He still felt shaky.

He began to walk. Moving would help him feel calm.

An hour later, Jack stood in front of his house. The lights were off. His parents were already sleeping.

Jack stepped inside. He moved quietly. He didn't want to wake his mom or dad. He didn't want to explain about Becky. About the police. They would find out soon enough. Besides, he felt tired. More tired than if he had run a marathon.

He changed. He got into bed. He thought he'd be sleeping in seconds. But he couldn't shut down his thoughts. He kept seeing Becky's body. The ambulance. Officers Breen and Dale. In his mind, they were giants. They towered over him. They peered down at him. Threatened him. Almost like the bullies back in elementary school.

He tossed and turned. Maybe he dozed off. He wasn't sure. The hours ticked by. The sun rose. Jack sat up. He still had time before his parents woke up.

He put on shorts and a T-shirt. He laced up his running shoes. Grabbed a sweatshirt. Then he slipped out of the house.

The streets were empty. Jack ran his regular loop around the lake. But he still had energy. So he went on to Lake Park, running through woods that circled the fields.

He kept his mind blank. He didn't want to think. Finally, he neared his street. He turned the corner and skidded to a stop. A police car was parked in front of his house. What was going on? Quickly, Jack ducked behind a bush. He peered out.

Breen and Dale walked up the steps. They rang the bell. After a moment his mom opened the door.

Jack moved from the bush to a tree to the car in the driveway. Each time, he hid for a second. Then he moved on. He reached the side of his house. He crept along. He was getting closer to his mom and the police. But was he close enough to listen in?

First he heard mumbles. He strained to hear. He caught some words. His name. Becky's name. Something about asking more questions. About going to the police station.

His mother gasped. Some of her words carried.

"Still sleeping."

"Wake him."

He heard the shock in her voice.

Jack gulped. His mom waved at the officers to come inside. They disappeared through the door.

Jack stood still. He couldn't move a muscle. But his heart pounded like crazy.

What should he do? He could go inside. Talk to his parents. Leave with the police. But what would he say? He already told them everything he knew. And what if he did talk? His words might be twisted. Misunderstood. He could be arrested. Found guilty.

Who knew what would happen?

Jack was never good at explaining. Even when the told the truth, he sounded like a liar. But he was good at one thing. Running.

He took off.

Jack raced through backyards. He jumped fences. He stayed off streets. He kept out of sight.

He ran and ran. He lost track of time. There was only the sound of his feet pounding. His heart beating. He kept going. And then he couldn't run anymore.

Jack was on the edge of town, between some warehouses. He leaned against a tree, panting. Where should he go? What should he do?

He was wearing shorts and a T-shirt. He had his old track sweatshirt tied around his waist. He had no other clothes. No money. Just a watch to time his run.

But he had to keep going. Had to stay on the run. He couldn't go home. His parents would make him go to the police station.

He couldn't talk to the police! He couldn't!

"I need to think," Jack told himself. "Figure things out. I am innocent." He stood up straight.

"And I will prove it."

CHAPTER 6

A NEW LOOK

First Jack had to find a place to hide. *An empty house would be nice,* he thought. He could sleep. Get his act together.

Are any friends out of town? On vacation?

Tim Hayes! He was away with his family. His house wasn't too far away. It would be perfect.

Once again, Jack took off. He reached the house in no time. It was still early in the morning. There were no neighbors around. Good.

Jack checked the driveway. No cars. That was

good too. They really were away. Now he just had to get inside.

Jack went to every door. He turned every knob. They were all locked, of course. But one window was open just a bit. It was on the ground floor. It should be easy to get in that way.

Jack pushed the window up higher. He jumped a bit. Then he wriggled through the opening.

He fell onto the floor and scrambled to his feet. He was in the living room. No! He remembered Tim had a dog. What if he was here?

"Here, boy," Jack called softly. "It's only me. A friend!"

Jack didn't hear barks or growls. *No dog*, he thought. *The family must have taken him. These are all good signs. An open window. No dog. Things are going my way.*

Still, it felt weird to be in Tim's house. The place was so quiet. Jack's footsteps echoed. He went into the kitchen. He ate some cereal and a banana. Then he wandered around. He saw a group picture on the piano. It was his old soccer team. He and Tim stood in the center.

Jack looked at the photo more closely. The two were the same height. And they had the same kind of build. They were the exact same size. They must be about the same size now too. Tim's clothes would fit him.

Jack grinned. Things were really going his way. He hurried to Tim's room. He opened drawers. He went through the closet. Jeans. Shorts. Shirts. He could have his pick. And in the sock drawer, he found a bunch of twenty-dollar bills.

"I'll pay you back, Tim," Jack said out loud. "And I'll wash all your clothes and return them."

Next step: a shower. In the bathroom, Jack discovered something else he could use. Hair dye!

He could change his hair color. It would be a disguise. If he looked different enough, no one would know him. He wouldn't have to sneak everywhere. He could walk down the street like a regular person.

Jack read the instructions on the box. A half hour later, he had dark, almost black, hair. But he still looked like Jack Porter.

Next, Jack took a pair of scissors. He cut off his bangs. He trimmed all around. He peered in the mirror. It was a terrible haircut. Ragged and messy. But he looked so different! Now if he could find some glasses. That would make it perfect.

Jack searched in desks and on shelves. In the study, he found an old pair. He slipped them on. Things were just a tiny bit blurry. But he could see fine.

He laughed. Not even his parents would recognize him!

Then Jack got organized. He found a back-pack. He got paper and pen. A sleeping bag. Soap, a toothbrush, and toothpaste. He brought over the clothes and the money. And he packed it all up.

By now, Jack was bone-tired. He fell into Tim's bed. In seconds, he was fast asleep.

Morning turned to afternoon, afternoon to night. Jack slept on, hour after hour.

Finally, a noise woke him. The front door opened, then slammed shut. A dog barked.

"It's six in the morning!" he heard Tim say. He sounded angry. "Why did we leave in the middle of the night? To miss traffic? We could have had an extra day away!"

The family argued in the front hall. Then they moved into the kitchen.

Jack grabbed the backpack. He tiptoed down the stairs. And he slipped outside.

CHAPTER 7

I AM INNOCENT

Jack strolled down the streets of his hometown. Lake was waking up. In the town center he sat on a bench. It was a Sunday like any other Sunday. People pushed strollers. They stopped in stores. They greeted friends. No one gave him a second look.

Jack felt like a different person. New hair. New glasses. New clothes.

Same old problem. He was wanted for murder.

He took out the paper and pen from his backpack.

Dear Mom and Dad,
Try not to worry. I am doing OK.
I am innocent, I swear.
Love, Jack

He hurried to his house. He made sure no one was around. Then he put the note in the mailbox.

One thing done, he told himself. *Now what*?

Jack needed to prove his innocence. He just didn't know how. But now he had time. Somehow, he'd come up with a plan.

All that week, Jack slept in empty garages. He hung out in parks. He went to the mall. He didn't do much. He sat. He napped. He walked. If he saw someone he knew? He ducked out of sight.

He spent his days wandering and thinking. Often, he went to his favorite hangout, the Coffee Stop. He never looked anyone in the eye.

One afternoon he smiled at the server without thinking. She was a junior at East Lake. Jack knew her name, Kim. They had sat next to each other at lunch. But she acted like she didn't know him. "Large coconut iced coffee with double whipped cream." She didn't blink. "Coming up."

Jack left soon after. He walked down the street, lost in thought. Did he look that different? Kim had no idea who he was. But maybe she wasn't paying attention. Maybe someone else would recognize—

Jack knocked into someone's shoulder.

"Watch it, young man!" a man cried.

Jack raised his head. He drew in his breath. "Mr. Scott!" he said in surprise. He'd just bumped into his old math teacher. Really, bumped right into him!

Jack groaned. He'd almost failed that class. Math was not his best subject. Plus Mr. Scott didn't like him. And that made it worse.

Now, Jack wished he could take back his words. Why did he have to say the teacher's name? It had just popped out! He couldn't help it. But would the teacher know Jack? Recognize his voice? Call the police?

"Be more careful," Mr. Scott grumbled. He turned his back and walked away.

Yes, Jack realized. *I really do look different.*

He could walk right up to people he knew. Say hello. And they wouldn't know him. Still, he should watch out for his parents. Surely they'd know him. No matter what.

Every day, Jack left a note for them at his house. Each time, Jack made sure no one was home. Then he'd slip the paper into the mailbox.

Everything is OK. I love you, Jack.

It was always hard to see his home. His bedroom window. The old swing set in the backyard.

Part of Jack just wanted to stay there. To crawl into his own bed, with his own stuff. To know his parents would watch out for him. Take care of him.

Would that be so bad? he wondered. *To dump my problems on them? And see if they could fix everything?*

But Jack knew that wouldn't be right. He didn't want to drag them into it. Not if he could fix everything himself.

It was Wednesday, almost a week since the murder. Jack went to the Coffee Stop. He got his usual coffee. Then he sat at a corner table.

Someone had left the town newspaper. The *Weekly Lake.* He glanced at the front page.

His face stared back at him. It was his class picture. And Becky's photo was next to it.

Jack read the headline, "A Murder and a Mystery. Did Jack Porter Kill Becky Mann?"

Jack wanted to scream, "No!" He wanted to rip the newspaper to shreds. But he had to stay calm.

He sipped the coffee. He took deep breaths. Then he read the article. Maybe it would give him an idea. A plan to find the real killer. Clear his name.

Quickly, he skimmed the first sentences. Senior at East. Junior at West. School dance. Then he read more slowly. The reporter had talked to students. Did people think he was guilty?

"I don't know," Tim Hayes said. "I mean, people do crazy things."

A girl named Dawn said, "We were in bio together. He cut through a frog like it was a slice of bread!"

"He has a mean streak," a boy named Ben said. *A mean streak?* Jack didn't even know the kid. "He has to have one. Otherwise, he couldn't win all those races."

Jack closed his eyes. This couldn't be real! He kept reading.

The reporter quoted Luke next. "Jack is innocent," his old friend said. "He has never hurt anyone. Ever. He's too nice a guy. It has to be someone else."

Well, one person is on my side, Jack thought. It just didn't feel like enough.

CHAPTER 8

THE FUNERAL

Jack tossed the newspaper in the garbage. He felt so angry! He kicked the table leg. Then he left the Coffee Stop.

On the street he didn't know where to turn. It was so unfair! Rage boiled inside him. He needed to get the anger out. He needed to run. But he couldn't just take off. People would stare at him. And he had a way of running, a special kind of form. Someone might say, "Hey! Jack Porter runs like that!"

Jack had to hold in his feelings. He had to wait to run.

Instead, he stomped down the street. He passed a candy store, then the post office, then another store. Suddenly he stopped in front of a window. A dozen TVs faced the street. His face was on each one of them.

"Have you seen this man?" read the line underneath.

Jack groaned. It was even worse than the newspaper.

Then his face disappeared. A funeral came on screen. Jack couldn't move. He couldn't tear his eyes away. He'd been feeling sorry for himself. Sorry that he couldn't run. But of course, there was poor Becky. She would never run again. Ever.

And her family …

A man and woman stepped out of a black car. Her parents, Jack thought. They bowed their heads. Then they walked slowly into the church. Jack swallowed. It was hard to watch.

Next, the camera zoomed in on a boy and a girl.

They stood side by side. Another line read, "Boyfriend and best friend."

Jack gasped. Becky had a boyfriend?

He thought back. He didn't walk over to Becky. She walked over to him. She had started talking. She started flirting.

But she had a boyfriend! Why did she flirt with Jack? And why did she go to the dance?

And then Jack had another thought. Did that have something to do with her murder?

The boyfriend and best friend looked upset. They leaned against one another. The girl stumbled. The boy helped her inside the church. Jack stared at their faces. They looked like regular kids. People he might have passed on the street. But he had to remember them. He had to be able to pick them out of a crowd.

A commercial came on.

Jack turned away. He had more questions than

ever before. But now he had an idea. A way to get answers.

That boy and girl knew Becky. They all had a past together. He would start with the boy. He'd find him. He'd find out what he was like.

What was his plan? Go to West Lake High. And search.

CHAPTER 9

WEST LAKE UNDERCOVER

The next morning Jack was up with the sun. It was already hot. He had slept at Lake Park, inside a soccer net. Somehow, it felt safe there. Like the net gave him cover.

Jack changed into clean clothes. Then he packed up everything. Wrappers from a deli. A bottle of water. His toothbrush.

He hurried out of the park and onto the street. He peered at a car window, using it like a mirror. He sighed. He didn't look great. But he looked all right. Not like a crazed killer at least. He could pass for a regular student. He shouldered his backpack.

He was off to school.

A few blocks later, the street grew crowded. Up ahead, Jack saw West Lake High. Car after car pulled up to the front. Tons of kids spilled out.

"Coming through. Coming through!" A crowd of boys pushed past Jack. Kids swarmed around him.

West had the same feel as East. Some kids hurried. Some just hung out. But it was weird. Jack didn't know anyone. And he didn't know anything about the school. He'd never been inside.

Slowly, Jack walked into the lobby. No one said hello. No one even smiled. He felt invisible. He peered around at the faces. He didn't see the boyfriend or the best friend. At least he didn't think so. Maybe they looked different at the funeral. They'd be wearing shorts now, or jeans. Not a black suit or a dress.

The bell rang. Kids rushed off. In seconds, he was alone.

"Get to class!" one teacher told him. Jack nodded.

Uh-oh, he thought. *I better find somewhere to go.* He wandered down a hall. All the classroom doors were closed.

He kept walking. Then he spied the boys' locker room. He poked his head in. No one was there. In one corner, he found an empty locker. He stood in front of it. And he pretended to put stuff away.

I can just keep doing this, he thought. *Then I can walk the halls between classes.* All the kids would be out then. He'd search faces. Then during class, he'd come back to the locker room.

The morning passed. Lunch blocks were starting. Everyone headed in the same direction. They were going to the cafeteria.

Jack let people edge around him. But one boy walked against the crowd. People parted for him.

They looked at him without seeming to look. They shook their heads sadly.

"There goes Rob," a boy whispered. No one spoke to him.

Right away, Jack knew it was the boyfriend.

Rob, the boyfriend, stepped past Jack. Jack could have reached out and touched him. Quietly, Jack turned. He followed him. Up one hall, down another.

Rob stopped. In a flash Jack ducked back around the corner. He peered around the wall. Rob scanned the hall. *He's making sure no one is here,* Jack realized. *That no one sees where he's going.*

Rob opened a classroom door. He disappeared inside.

Jack waited. No one else walked past. So he crept along to the classroom. He walked past the door Rob used. There was another door at the end of the hall. Just as Jack thought, it was a second door to the same room.

He snuck a peek through the window. Rob

wasn't alone. A girl was with him. They were standing, leaning against the teacher's desk. Jack could only see her back. She had curly blonde hair. The best friend had curly blonde hair too. It had to be her!

The two talked. Jack couldn't hear what they said. Minutes passed. Jack shifted. How long could he stand here before someone passed? He wasn't even learning anything!

Then the girl squeezed Rob's arm. Rob leaned forward. They kissed. They straightened, ready to leave.

Jack backed away from the door. He pressed against the back wall. The girl opened the far door and stepped out. Just then the bell rang.

Another girl hurried over. "Tessa!" she called. "I've been looking for you everywhere!"

Suddenly the hall filled with students. Rob came out. He turned left. Right away, he was lost in the crowd.

Meanwhile, Jack didn't move. *They kissed*!

he thought. *They're more than friends! Rob and Tessa. Boyfriend and best friend. And boyfriend and girlfriend.*

They were a couple.

But they were keeping it secret. Did they have something to hide? Were they together before Becky died? Or did it happen after?

Jack could see how that could happen. Someone close to them died. They were two people, sad beyond belief. They comforted each other. Their friendship deepened. Then they became more than friends.

Which was it? Romantic feelings before Becky was killed? Or after?

For the rest of the day, Jack hung out in the cafeteria. When school ended, he waited by the front door. Hopefully, Rob would leave that way. Jack squinted. He took off his fake glasses to see just a bit better.

Yes! There he was.

Walking alone, Rob left school. Jack followed a few paces behind.

Jack stayed behind Rob. He kept his distance. But he kept him in sight at all times. Together, they walked for around ten blocks. Finally, Rob turned down a street.

Jack waited. Then he turned down too.

Hmmm, thought Jack. *This looks familiar*.

Rob went into a yellow house. It stood next door to a large brick home.

Jack stared at the brick house. It was Becky's!

Rob and Becky were next-door neighbors. Then Jack remembered something. A window slamming closed while he waited for Becky.

Did Rob see Jack and Becky the night of the dance? Did he see Becky lean close to Jack? Whisper to him? Was he jealous? Did it make him crazy?

Crazy enough to kill?

CHAPTER 10

A FRIEND TO TRUST

Jack backed away. He turned down one street, then another.

Maybe I should stick with Rob, he thought. *Keep following him. Rob might meet up with Tessa again. Maybe Rob will confess.*

Jack didn't think so. But what if it did happen? Jack wouldn't see it. Wouldn't hear it. But right now, he needed a break.

After a while, Jack found himself at the Coffee Stop. He had to smile. He wasn't planning it. He wasn't planning anything at all. His body just brought him here. He must need a coffee.

Inside, he ordered his usual. "Large coconut iced coffee with double whipped cream."

Suddenly someone grabbed his arm. "Jack! It's you," a boy hissed in his ear.

Jack's heart dropped. He wanted to run. But whoever this was, Jack had to face him. He would deny he was Jack Porter. He would say his name was Tom. Or Alex. Or Ronald McDonald. Whatever it took. He'd say he must look like this other guy. He forced himself to turn.

It was Luke.

"Oh!" Jack said, surprised. He couldn't pretend he was someone else. Not with Luke.

"I knew it!" Luke said. "Who else would order that?"

He pulled Jack over to a table. "Tell me everything," he said.

Jack took off the glasses. "Well," he began. "I—"

"You forgot this." The server brought over his coffee. Jack quickly put the glasses back on. "Thank you."

He gazed at Luke. Should he trust him? He and Luke went way back. Luke had told the reporter that Jack was innocent. But still, Jack could see Luke's cell phone in his shirt pocket. He just had to take it out. Dial three numbers, 9-1-1. And the police would be there in seconds.

"Why should I stay here?" he asked Luke. "You could turn me in." He got out of his seat.

Luke blocked his way. "Don't go anywhere!" He looked Jack in the eye. "Please. I know you, Jack. I know you wouldn't kill anyone. And maybe I can help you."

It was true. Luke was smart. He could have some ideas. Some new thoughts.

Jack sat back down. For a moment he was quiet. After so many days on his own. So many days of not talking. It was hard to open up.

"The police want me for murder." His voice

was hoarse. He'd hardly spoken for a week. "I'm on the run. My only chance is to find the real killer." Jack paused. "Before the police find me."

"See?" Luke smiled. "I knew I could help. We can work as a team. Tell me more."

Jack talked for an hour. About hiding out. About following Rob. It felt good to let it all out.

"Okay, here's what I think," Luke told him. "You keep following Rob. I'll follow Tessa. Those two? They're our best bet. And with me working too? It will take you half the time."

Jack sighed. It felt good to have someone else make a decision.

"Come with me now," Luke went on. "We'll go to my house. Get more supplies."

First, Luke made sure no one was home. Then he brought Jack inside. They went to his room. Jack stretched out on the bed. A real bed! Soft and comfortable. It felt like a gift.

"Don't fall asleep," Luke warned. "My mom will be home any minute."

Jack leaped up.

"It's okay." Luke laughed. "Let me get some stuff for you. You go shower."

Seconds later, Jack stood under a stream of water. His muscles relaxed. His whole body felt better. He wanted to stay there forever.

After, Luke gave him two striped T-shirts. "I'd give you more. But my mom would notice," he said.

Jack pulled one on. It was a little small. It pulled at his shoulders. But it felt clean and fresh. Really amazing. He smiled happily. Most of his clothes were damp from rain and dew. They smelled funny too. Strange how a clean shirt could make you feel so good. Usually, you just took it for granted.

Then Luke tossed him a key. "This is for my bike lock. Take my bike. It's in the garage. The helmet is on the seat."

"Thanks!" Jack said. He was about to say more. But Luke handed him a big roll of cash. "What?" said Jack. "How much money is here?"

Luke shrugged. "Don't worry about it. I know you'll pay me back. You should ride to another town. Maybe Greenfield. Buy more clothes. It would be safer there. No one knows you." He grinned at Jack. "Hey! You can get breakfast at the Coffee Stop there. It's next door to a clothing store called the Rack. After you eat, get some new shorts and stuff."

It all made sense. "Okay," Jack said. "I'll go to Greenfield first thing in the morning. What time does the Rack open?"

Luke checked his computer. "Ten in the morning. Plenty of time for breakfast before."

Jack smiled. "It's a plan" He thumped Luke on the back. "Thanks again, bud."

For the first time since the dance, Jack relaxed. He felt hopeful.

He had a friend.

CHAPTER 11

A POLICE TIP

That night, Jack slept in a garage. It was just a block from Luke's house. He was walking past it when he saw the family. They were packing a giant SUV with sleeping bags and backpacks and coolers.

Another lucky break, Jack thought. They were going away. And their garage? It was big enough for two giant SUVs. Maybe three. Half the garage had carpet on the floor. There was a chair. Even a refrigerator! It was cool and comfortable. Jack slept and slept.

Finally, he woke with a start. "Wow!" he said. It was past nine. And he actually felt good! Wide awake and ready.

He stuffed his things into the backpack. He put on the helmet. Then he took off on Luke's bike. He checked his watch. It should take an hour to get to Greenfield.

At ten o'clock, Jack reached the Coffee Stop. Just as Luke said, the Rack was next door. As Jack watched, a worker unlocked the door.

Jack's stomach growled. He was hungry. He should eat first, like he and Luke had agreed. But there was a line at the Coffee Stop. And after riding an hour, the small striped shirt was really uncomfortable. He could shop quickly. Buy some things. It would only take a little while.

Jack locked up his bike by the Coffee Stop. Then he walked into the Rack.

Inside, he picked out shirts, shorts, under-wear, and socks. Even a new pair of sneakers. Did he need anything else?

"Let's see," Jack said out loud. He opened his backpack and went through his things. Where was his sweatshirt? He loved that sweatshirt! It was his East Lake High track sweatshirt. It had his name on it.

It was gone.

Jack felt bad. Like he'd lost something special. But he shrugged it off. It was just a sweatshirt after all. Other people had lost much more. He grabbed a Greenfield sweatshirt from a shelf. He paid for everything.

When he left the store, he was wearing his new clothes. *Much better,* he thought. *Now it's breakfast time.*

The Coffee Stop had only a few customers. "Next?" called a server.

Jack stepped up to the counter. He opened his mouth to order. But a siren sounded. He turned to look out the window. A police car screeched to a stop outside.

Two police officers jumped out. Oh no! It was Breen and Dale. Now what? They rushed into the Coffee Stop.

Jack's heart thudded. It was so loud. He thought everyone could hear it. He edged away from the counter. He pressed against the wall. How small could he make himself?

Not small enough, he knew. He was only inches from the officers.

The officers bowed their heads toward each other. They spoke in low voices. But Jack was close. He could hear every word.

"The tip may be right," Dale said. "Porter could be here. Or somewhere close-by."

Tip? Jack said to himself. *Someone called the police? Told them to look in the Coffee Stop?*

Breen glanced at Jack. Her eyes slid right past him, still searching.

"The bike is outside. Just like the guy said." She looked down at a pad. "Porter should be wearing a striped T-shirt."

Dale shook his head. "That could be any bike. I tell you, Porter's not here. It's just another crazy caller. Sending us on another wild goose chase. Remember when we searched that mall forty miles away? I'm done."

"Yup." Breen agreed. "We should just leave. The search is on hold anyway. We don't have enough on Porter. At least that's what the captain said."

The two kept talking. Jack took a deep breath. Then he nodded at the officers and walked right past them. A second later he was outside. Safe.

For now.

CHAPTER 12

BETRAYAL

Jack walked away from the Coffee Stop. He left the bike on the ground. It might still be a target. Better to get around on two feet.

He started to jog. His backpack bounced. The sidewalk was cracked and uneven. And he had miles to go. But that was okay. Moving helped him think.

First thing he decided. Find Luke. Explain what happened. How he heard the search was called off. Good news, he thought.

Wait! Jack stopped in the middle of the

sidewalk. His heart sank. Why did the police go to Greenfield? To the Coffee Stop there? How did they know he had a bike? That he would be wearing a striped T-shirt?

Luke was the only one who knew. He must have told them.

Why?

Luke thought he was guilty! He wanted Jack to be caught. His one friend didn't think he was innocent after all.

A little girl bumped into him. "Oops!" she said.

"Sorry," said her mom. She picked up her daughter and kept walking.

Jack shook his head to clear it. Standing here wouldn't help. He walked. Then jogged. Then ran.

He still had to get to Luke. He had to make him see the truth. That he didn't kill Becky.

Jack checked his watch. It was Friday, noon. Luke would be in school all afternoon. He would probably stay late to work on the newspaper too.

That was okay. Jack could be patient. There was so much at stake. Luke had to believe him. He had to!

Back in East Lake, the sun set. Evening fell. The streets grew dark. Jack circled Luke's home.

Jack knew Luke was there. Jack had been waiting. Hiding behind an old playhouse in the backyard. He wanted to get to Luke before he walked inside. To pull him aside and talk. But Luke had come home with his mom.

Did Jack dare go in? He knew the backdoor was open. He could sneak up the stairs. Make his way to Luke's room.

No. He couldn't take the chance. Too many people were around. Why now? Jack wondered. All of a sudden, it seemed Luke and his family were popular. The doorbell rang. People came and left. It was as busy as the town library.

Finally, Jack gave up. He found a spot in the

garage behind a pile of tires. It smelled of rubber. A draft came through the cracked window. But he felt safe. No one would look back there.

He took out his sleeping bag. By now he could fall asleep anywhere. In a park. In an empty lot. He closed his eyes. It would happen in seconds, he thought. Sleep. Instant relief from stress.

Jack waited. But once again, his brain wouldn't shut down. There was something worrying him. A nagging thought. He couldn't put his finger on it. Something about Luke.

Finally, his mind went blank. He slept.

Jack dreamed he was running. He was at the school track, leading a pack of runners. Soon all the runners faded away. Except one. One pair of footsteps thudded behind him. The runner was getting closer and closer. The footsteps pounded louder and louder.

Jack felt scared. Too scared to turn around, to see who was there. If he did, he would slow down.

Get caught. So he kept running. Now the runner was at his elbow. At his side.

Jack glanced to his right. It was Luke. But it didn't look like Luke. Not really. This Luke's hair was long and wild. It blew in all directions. His eyes were bloodshot. His mouth curved in a crazy grin.

"Gotcha!" Luke cried.

Jack woke up. Sweat drenched his back. His breath came in short bursts. It was like he'd really been running.

And then it came to him. That nagging thought. The idea he couldn't pin down.

If Luke thought he was the killer? Why did he let him into his home? Into his room?

Why wasn't he afraid?

CHAPTER 13

TWO MYSTERIES

Jack had a bad taste in his mouth. Nightmares did that to him. They soured his breath.

He brushed his teeth. Then he rinsed with water from a water bottle. It was six on Saturday morning. Jack looked out the garage window. Luke's house was quiet. He couldn't see movement or hear noise.

Jack ducked back behind the tires. He waited.

Now there are two mysteries, he thought.

Mystery number one, the murder. Mystery number two, what's the deal with Luke?

What made him call the police? Jack wondered. *Did he think I actually killed Becky? Or did he have some other reason?*

One hour crawled by. *Thump*! Jack heard a noise. The newspaper must have hit the front steps. He heard the door creak open.

Finally, people were up.

If Luke's parents went out, he would go inside. He would find Luke.

If Luke left first, he would follow him. Find a place where they could be alone. Hash everything out.

Jack felt confused about Luke. But he had to believe Luke was still his friend. He had nothing else to believe in.

Another hour passed slowly. Again, the door opened. Jack peeked out. He could see someone walking down the street. Luke.

Jack grabbed his stuff and followed.

He didn't want to stop Luke just anywhere. Luke could call for help. Say Jack was a killer.

He had to see where Luke was going. Then he'd figure out a plan.

It was cool and sunny. Lots of people were out. Jack moved around kids and dogs and moms and dads. He kept half a block behind Luke. He could see Luke fine. But Luke had no idea Jack was there.

I'm getting good at this, Jack thought. *Maybe I should be a detective.* He paused. *Or a criminal.*

Fifteen minutes later, Luke turned into Lake Park. So did Jack. Only a few nights ago, Jack had slept here. Now, the park hummed with action.

Kids in uniform ran in all directions. Every soccer field was taken. Parents sat on chairs on the sidelines. Or they paced up and down, following the game. Cheers and cries filled the air.

Jack lost sight of Luke.

A soccer ball rolled up to him. He tossed it to a player.

"Thank you," she said.

Then she threw it onto the field. The ref blew his whistle. "Both feet on the ground," he told the girl. "Try again."

The ref was young. A high school student, Jack thought. He looked closer.

It was Rob.

Jack grinned.

Luke must have found out Rob was a referee. And that he'd be working here today. Working. Luke was trying to find clues to the murder!

Maybe Luke didn't call the police. Maybe someone else did. And maybe he was still on Jack's side.

Rob blew the whistle again. Halftime. Kids wandered off the field.

Jack peered around. He wanted to find Luke. He needed to talk to him. Right now!

Wait! Was that Luke at the edge of the park? Over by the woods? Jack strolled over, trying to look like a regular guy in the park.

Weee-oh! Weee-oh! Police sirens blared.

Jack froze. *Hide*! he thought. It was a gut feeling. Already his feet were moving. He ducked into the woods.

The light dimmed. The air felt damp. The woods were quiet. The soccer games seemed far away.

Did the police cars pass?

Jack poked his head out between two trees. Players milled around the field. They were waiting for Rob, the ref. Jack didn't see him anywhere. Or Luke. He was about to step out and search. But then he heard something behind him. Deeper in the woods.

Crack! Branches snapped. *Thud*! *Crash*! There was a grunt and a groan. It sounded like a struggle. Like someone needed help.

"Oh!" cried a voice. Was that Luke? Was he with Rob?

Pictures flashed in Jack's mind. Rob killing Becky. Rob killing again. Luke could be in danger!

Jack took off.

CHAPTER 14

CALL THE POLICE!

Jack raced deep into the woods. The sounds grew louder. "Oof!" someone groaned. There was another crash, louder this time.

Jack pushed through branches. He ran around trees. Ahead, he saw a clearing. An open space. Two guys rolled on the ground. First one was on top, then the other. That's all Jack could tell. Maybe it wasn't Luke after all. Maybe this was none of his business.

Then one guy pinned the other. The one on top grabbed a sweatshirt. He wrapped it around the other guy's neck. The other guy struggled. He clawed at the sweatshirt. But he was too weak. He was choking!

Jack couldn't just stand there.

He rushed over. Then he gasped.

Luke was one guy. Rob was the other.

And Luke was on top. He was choking Rob!

Jack pulled at Luke. He gripped his shoulders and yanked. Hard. Luke fell off. The sweatshirt loosened.

Rob gagged. His face was bright red. He held his hands to his neck and rubbed.

Jack turned to face him. "Are you—" he began.

All at once, Luke jumped on Jack. Jack threw him off. Then he kneeled on Luke's back. He twisted his arm so he couldn't move.

"You okay?" he called to Rob again.

Rob nodded.

"Can you call the police?"

Rob took his phone from his shorts pocket. Seconds later, Jack heard sirens again. Soon, officers crowded into the clearing. They took hold of Luke.

"I don't know what's going on!" Rob told them. He pointed to Luke. "This crazy guy tried to kill me!"

He kicked at a sweatshirt. "He was choking me. With this!"

"I can explain." Jack stepped forward. The pieces were falling into place. Mysteries #1 and #2 were connected. And he had an idea why.

"My name is Jack Porter."

The police officers moved toward him. One took out his gun.

"Wait. Please." Jack spoke in a calm voice. He picked up the sweatshirt. It was his track team sweatshirt.

He pointed to Luke. "This is Luke Casey. He took my sweatshirt. He was using it as a weapon.

He wanted to frame me for murder. First Becky Mann's." He slowly turned to Rob. "And now her boyfriend's."

Rob nodded.

The officer in charge nodded too. "That may be. But you all need to go to the station."

Everyone left the clearing.

But only Luke wore handcuffs.

CHAPTER 15

GRADUATION DAY

Jack stood at the starting line. Once again he was on his high school track. But there was no meet. Seats had been set up in the infield. A stage stood at one end. It was East Lake graduation.

The seniors gathered in a group, Jack among them. Together, they marched to seats. People kept stepping out of line to see Jack. They clapped him on the back. They said they were glad he was there. Happy he was cleared. Tim Hayes gave him a thumbs-up. Jack had paid back the money and returned the clothes.

Jack mumbled his thanks. He wished everyone would just forget the whole thing. But how could they? It was all over the news.

Finally, Jack sat down.

A hush fell over the crowd. "Welcome, students, teachers, families, and friends," the principal said. He talked some more. He introduced other speakers. Jack didn't pay much attention. Instead, he replayed everything that had happened.

Becky's murder. Running away. Hiding. Discovering Rob and Tessa. Trusting Luke. Luke choking Rob.

The questions at the police station. And finally, the answers.

Luke was jealous of Jack. He hated Jack's success. That Jack had moved on, and that he was a track star. The final straw? That pretty Becky Mann seemed to like him.

Luke wanted Jack to suffer. He wanted people to think Jack Porter was a killer.

So Luke killed Becky. But it wasn't enough. The police gave up their search. There was no evidence. Luke wanted them to keep after Jack. So he took Jack's sweatshirt. Then he used it to try and kill Rob. But of course, he was caught. And the truth came out.

Right now Luke sat in jail. He was waiting for his trial. And Jack was at their high school graduation.

He was free.

Pictures were flashing on a giant screen behind the speaker. School plays. Concerts.

A shot of the newspaper room. Luke was front and center. Everyone gasped.

Heads turned toward Jack

"You were so brave," the girl next to him whispered.

"And smart," a boy leaned over to say. "You caught him."

Jack turned red. He never felt brave. Or smart. The only thing he did was show up at the right time and place. But maybe that was enough.

Still, he was glad when the band started to play. People faced the stage again. The students stood. They marched out.

High school was over.

Kids were looking for their families. Families were looking for their kids. Jack craned his neck. He peered all around.

Then the crowd parted. "Make way," someone whispered. "They want to see Jack."

Rob and Tessa walked toward him.

"Hey," Jack said. The three moved to the side.

"We came to say congratulations," Tessa said. "You've been through a lot."

"Yeah." Rob hugged him. "We're here for you. Just like you were for me. You saved my life, man."

By now, Jack knew their story too.

Rob had broken up with Becky. But no one

knew. Becky wanted to keep it secret. She thought she could change his mind.

Her plan? Have Rob see her with another guy. Then he'd come back. She picked Jack. She went to the dance with him. She knew Rob was home that night. And that he might be watching. So she kept Jack waiting. To give Rob time to see Jack outside his window. Then she leaned in close to Jack. She flirted.

And then at the dance? She couldn't care less. She'd gotten what she wanted.

"I knew Becky since kindergarten," Tessa had said. "We'd always been friends. But lately, she was not a good person."

"Jack! Jack!" voices called out.

"There are your parents," said Rob.

"Take care," said Tessa.

And they were gone.

Jack's parents hurried over. They took his picture. They made a fuss. They kissed him again and again.

Then Jack took off his cap and gown. Underneath, he had on shorts and a T-shirt. He handed the graduation clothes to his mom. He tied his sneakers.

He was ready to run.

"Not because I have to," he told himself. "Because I want to."

WANT TO KEEP READING?

9781680211061

Turn the page for a sneak
peek at another book in the
White Lightning series:

QWIK CUTTER

CHAPTER 1

FADE-IN

Get to class!" EJ's voice boomed.

EJ was the head security guard at Cube Middle School. He was tall and muscular. He wore work out clothes every day.

Seventh-grader Shawn Miller always heard his voice. If you were outside when class started, everyone heard it. You could be anywhere on campus. Some students said they could hear it inside the classrooms too.

Shawn was outside when class started. He was always late.

Today he had to stay behind after second period. He needed extra time to do his math test. He was unorganized. And he started the test late. By the time he got going, some kids were done.

Shawn's third period class was Advanced Video Production.

He loved it. He loved making movies. His favorite ones were horror films. He wanted to be a director some day. But he knew he would have to be more organized to see his dream come true.

Mr. Murphy, the video production teacher, was cool. He directed music videos when he wasn't working at Cube. He also uploaded his videos. The students could watch them on YouTube.

Still, as cool as he was, even Mr. Murphy got tired of Shawn always being late.

Shawn gritted his teeth as he sprinted across campus. He was sweating through his black T-shirt.

He hated that his second and third period classes were on opposite ends of the school.

Mr. Murphy won't care about that, he reminded himself.

Somehow he got to video production with five seconds to spare.

He barely heard anything Mr. Murphy said all period. He was working on his science homework. It was due the next period. It had been assigned three days ago. But that didn't matter. He was always late.

He liked the topic. Wormholes

He loved anything having to do with time travel. He enjoyed learning about outer space. One day he hoped to make a movie about it. He even wanted to shoot the movie in space.

Shawn eyed the clock. *Five more minutes,* he told himself. He just had a few more science questions to complete.

"Don't forget," Mr. Murphy said. "Your summer projects are due tomorrow."

This news normally made students groan. But this wasn't English class. Nobody in Advanced Video Production complained about projects. They all loved being in the class.

"You can either upload them tonight. Or turn them in on a DVD. Or a flash drive. Or an SD card."

"Summer project?" Shawn blurted out.

He was thankful his table partner, John Gomez, was the only one who heard him. John was Shawn's best friend. They had known each other since fourth grade. They both loved technology and making movies. Shawn loved to shoot movies. John loved to edit them. They planned to start a production company some day.

"Yeah," Amanda Nguyen said smartly behind her big black glasses. "Mr. Murphy has only been talking about it since forever. Duh!"

Shawn ignored her. She'd always hated him. He had called her "four eyes" in first grade. But that wasn't the reason why Amanda disliked him. It was because he never got in trouble. For being unorganized. For being late.

Studying late.

Turning in his assignments late.

Sure, he had to stay after class a lot. But his grades never suffered.

Amanda despised that about him. She was super organized. She was prepared. She was always on time. Always first to raise her hand.

The bell rang. Class was over.

"Have you started editing your project?" Shawn asked John.

"Yeah," John said as he slid his iPad into his backpack. "Haven't you?"

"What do you think?" Amanda snapped before he could answer. "Does Shawn Miller ever do anything on time? Does he ever do anything without having to be reminded to do it a million times?"

Amanda turned and left in a huff.

Shawn was used to her insults. He didn't

say anything back. He didn't have anything to say anyway.

"We shot all that footage over the summer," John said as he headed for the door. "You mean you haven't even started cutting it?"

"It was assigned too early," Shawn said. He walked out of the class with John. "I forgot about it."

"Well, it's due tomorrow. What are you gonna do?"

"I'll get it done." Shawn said confidently. "I always get it done."